Weldon Wexford and Murkle Monster go to WIZARD camp

written by David Ezra Spinner
pictures by Peggy Collins

For those with monster-sized dreams.
Never let go of your imagination.
Always remember you are pure MAGIC!
-David Ezra Spinner

weldonandmurkle@gmail.com.

weldonandmurkle.com

Illustration and design by Peggy Collins

ISBN 978-0-9863085-2-9

*

First Edition

It's the last day of the school year and
we have a ceremony to celebrate.
I win the **Wizard of The Year** award.

I feel extra-ordinarily-magic-tastically AWESOME!

Murkle Monster helps hang my medal
on our wall of awards.

He slobbers ALL over them! GROSS!

Murkle Monster is my best friend.
We use our imaginations to find
adventures everywhere we go.

Murkle Monster and I are
extra-ordinarily-magic-tastically thrilled for our
NEW adventure. WIZARD CAMP!

Wizard camp is full of magical activities
where we can earn badges.

They will
look great on
my wall.

Murkle Monster
and I pack our trunks.

We bring
EVERYTHING!

My parents give us a care package and
hug us before we leave.
The gnomes wave to us from the backyard.
"We'll miss you," they say.

Murkle Monster and I board the bus from our chimney.
It soars across the sky.
The bus is extra-ordinarily-magic-tastically fast!

We spot a flock of
phoenix in the clouds.
They are brilliant!

I chew on magical candies from the trolley.
They turn my head into a pumpkin!

A wacky witch greets us
when we arrive.

"Welcome to wizard
camp," announces
Mrs. Broomswick.

She throws down
3 magic beans and
waves her wand
until they grow.

"Weldon Wexford
and Murkle Monster,
you'll be in the
beanstalk bunk"

We spiral up the beanstalk.
It is extra-ordinarily-magic-tastically tall!

The bunk quickly
fills up with more
campers.

Everyone introduces themselves.
We are all VERY different.

There is a calendar of magical activities on the door.
We are ready to earn our badges!

All the campers
meet Mrs. Broomswick
near the totem pole.

We listen carefully as she goes over the rules.

We put on our vests and begin our magical adventures.

Murkle Monster and I pitch the biggest tent.

We hit the most targets
during wand practice.

And mix the bubbliest potions
in our cauldron.

Earning badges is
extra-ordinarily-magic-
tastically easy!

Even the monsters have their own activities.

Murkle Monster finds the most slugs!

Murkle Monster
hatches the most
hooting owls.

They love him
SO MUCH!

Other wizards and witches are way behind during cloud canoe races.

Murkle Monster and I are on our way to victory!

During lunch we get a special snack but the monsters eat them before we can.

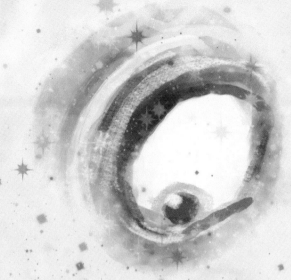

They all have

MONSTER FARTS!
EWWW!

My bunkmates and I laugh so hard!

I notice my friends are
extra-ordinarily-magic-tastically sad.

They are struggling to earn badges.

So I decide to
help them.

We track trolls during hiking. They are sneaky and hide very well.

Murkle Monster and I teach our bunkmates how to find them.

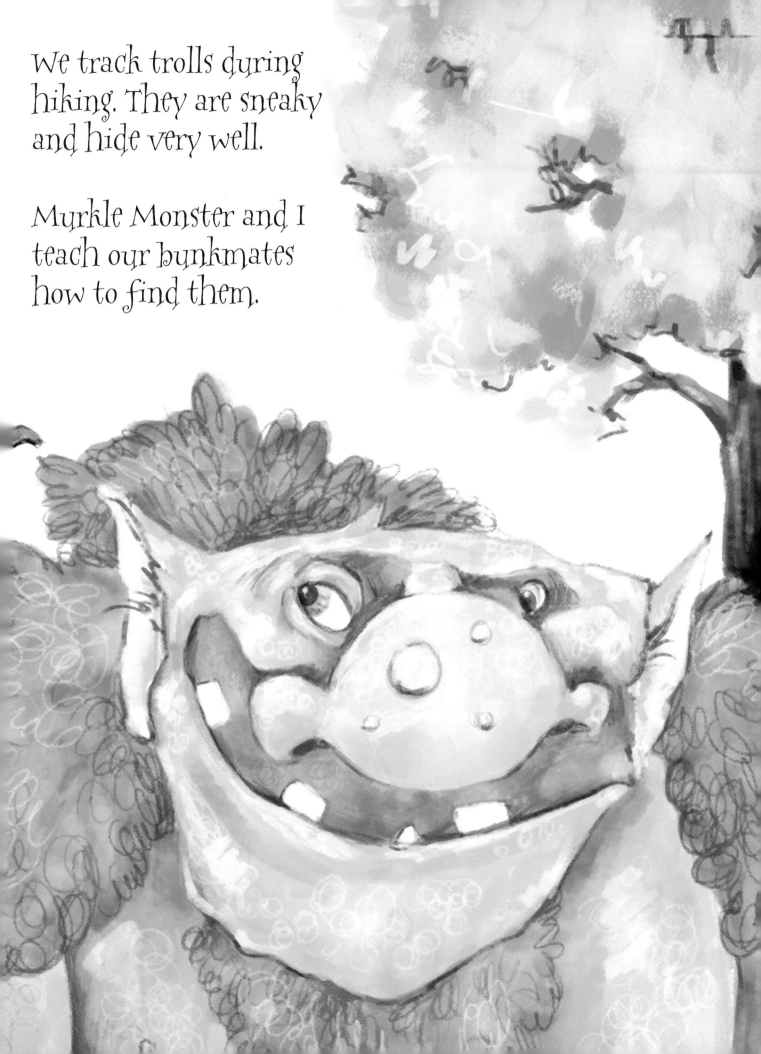

We show the campers how to ride their griffins around the ranch.

Everyone is doing extra-ordinarily-magic-tastically fantastic!

Star fishing turns out to be harder than I thought.
We motivate each other and work as a team.

The stars zip
and zoom
overhead and are
eventually caught.

"I've never played Capture the Cloak before," I tell my friends. So they teach me how to play!

We have SO much fun!

Everyone shows each other
their badges.

My friends and I celebrate with
gooey s'mores and tell ghost stories
around the mystical fire.
We stay up ALL NIGHT!

I tell my parents all about
WIZARD CAMP
when we come home.
They are very proud of us.

We earned a lot of badges but our
favorite part was making friends.

Murkle Monster and I hang a picture of our
bunkmates on the wall.
It is EXTRA-ORDINARILY-MAGIC-TASTICALLY
picture perfect!